Dear Parent,

Here is the perfect book to read to your child on a hot summer day!

As a little girl and her grandmother sit on the stoop of their apartment building talking about the heat, they realize it doesn't do any good to talk about the weather – they've got to do something about the heat. And what should they do? Why, go to the beach, of course! So the two of them board a stuffy train and head for the beach, where they enjoy all the things that make being at the ocean fun – salt air, building sand castles, licking ice-cream cones, and staying cool. As the sun goes down and the air begins to cool, they head back to the city and the end of a perfect day.

Stephanie Calmenson's exuberant text and Elivia Savadier's imaginative illustrations bring to life the warm relationship between grandmother and granddaughter and the fun of a special day they share together.

Sincerely,

Fritz J. Luecke
Editorial Director
Weekly Reader Book Club

Weekly Reader Children's Book Club Presents

Hotter Than a HOT DOG!

by **Stephanie Calmenson**

Illustrated by **Elivia**

Little, Brown and Company
Boston New York Toronto London

This book is a presentation of Newfield Publications, Inc.
Newfield Publications offers book clubs for children from
preschool through high school. For further information
write to: **Newfield Publications, Inc.,**
4343 Equity Drive, Columbus, Ohio 43228.

Published by arrangement with Little, Brown and Company (Inc.).
Newfield Publications is a federally registered trademark
of Newfield Publications, Inc. Weekly Reader is a federally
registered trademark of Weekly Reader Corporation.

First Edition

Library of Congress Cataloging-in-Publication Data

Calmenson, Stephanie.
    Hotter than a hot dog! / by Stephanie Calmenson ; illustrated by
Elivia Savadier. — 1st ed.
        p.   cm.
    Summary: A little girl and her grandmother escape the city on a
hot summer day by going to the beach.
    ISBN 0-316-12479-6
    [1. Beaches — Fiction. 2. Summer — Fiction. 3. Grandmothers —
Fiction.] I. Savadier, Elivia, ill. II. Title.
PZ7.C136Ho   1994
[E] — dc20   93-313

Printed in the United States of America

To my mother and father
—S. C.

For Laura and Sadye
and all the love
between them
—E. S.

Granny and I were sitting on our stoop, trying to decide who was hotter.

"I'm hotter than a hot dog in a campfire!" I said.

"I'm hotter than a salamander in the sun," said Granny.

"Hotter than a turkey in the oven!" I said. And I started trotting around the sidewalk like a big, fat turkey.

"Sit back down!" said Granny. "It's too hot to trot."

I sat down, then threw myself back.

"Look, Granny! I fainted!" I said.

"Emergency rescue!" called Granny. She took off her hat and waved it over me like a fan.

The breeze felt really good.

"Now it's your turn," I said.

I took Granny's hat and I waved it. I waved it so hard, there wasn't a breeze, there was a tornado!

"You're going to blow me away!" whooped Granny.

Honnnk! Honnnk! A truck driver was blowing his horn.
He wanted traffic to move faster.

A man walking by got a long string of pink gum stuck
to his shoe. "Darn!" he muttered.

People sure got cranky when it was hot. I was starting
to get a little cranky myself. I edged over to the shade,
but it didn't do any good.

"Granny, I'm so hot. What are we going to do?" I moaned.
Granny stood up.

"We're going!" she said.

"Where?" I asked.

"To the beach," said Granny.

Well, I wasn't too hot to jump for joy.

"Whoopee!!" I cried.

In no time our bags were packed and we were getting on the train. It swallowed us up like a fire-breathing dragon. It was ten times hotter than the stoop.

Looking out the window, I could see heat rising from the rooftops. The train was moving fast. It was shaking from side to side.

"Come sit next to me," said Granny. "It's a long ride."

My legs were hot and they stuck to the seat.

Suddenly we disappeared into a tunnel. It was dark. The train was rocking. I fell asleep.

The next thing I knew, Granny was shaking me awake.
"We're here," she said. The iron dragon opened its
jaws and spit us out into another world.

The sun was so bright I could hardly keep my eyes
open. And the air smelled different. Kind of salty.

The first thing I did when we got to the sand was kick off my shoes.

"Better wait!" warned Granny. Too late.

"Ouch! Ouch!" I cried. The sand was so hot, I felt like I had jumped into a frying pan.

I got my shoes back on fast. We walked down the beach till we found a spot we liked. The sand was a little cooler closer to the water.

Granny got down and started digging.

"Come help me," she said.

"What are we making?" I asked.

"You'll see," said Granny.

We dug two tunnels. One was as long as Granny. The other was as long as me. We pulled our blankets over the tunnels and Granny exclaimed, "Who needs to carry chairs?"

I plopped down in my sand chair and swished my body around till there were bumps in all the right places.

I didn't want to stay there very long though.

"I'm hot again," I said.

"We've got a big blue ocean to cool off in," said Granny.

"Last one in the water is a soggy noodle!" I called. I jumped up and ran.

When my feet hit the water, I cried, "Ouch! Ouch!" This time it felt like I had jumped into a bowl of ice cubes. But I loved it!

I raced in and dunked under. Finally I wasn't hot anymore.

The waves were just right — not big enough to be scary, but big enough to ride to shore.

Granny and I stayed in the water till our skin got all wrinkly.

"Let's take a walk and dry off," said Granny.
The air felt good on my wet skin. I skipped ahead, looking for treasures.

I found a starfish washed up on the shore. It was still alive, so I tossed it back into the water.

Then I found a scallop shell, and one perfect periwinkle shell.

"This one's for you, Granny," I said.

By the time we got back to the blanket, I was hot again. And thirsty. I saw people coming down from the boardwalk with ice-cream cones. My mouth started to water. My eyes opened wide.

"I know someone who wants ice cream," said Granny.

"Who's that?" I asked, as if I didn't know.

"Me!" said Granny with a big smile.

"Me too!" I said. But Granny already knew that.

I got strawberry ice cream. Granny got chocolate.

We had to eat our ice cream fast before it melted.

When we finished, my mouth was cool, but that was all. The rest of me was as hot as ever.

"Can we go in the water again?" I asked.

"I'd like to rest a little," said Granny. "Why don't you read your book to me?"

I had brought along the coolest one I could find. It was about a polar bear who lived at the North Pole. I read the book to Granny in my best polar bear voice.

"*'Wheee! This is fun!' said the polar bear, as she went slipping and sliding across the ice.*"

I made believe I was slipping and sliding right along with her. I forgot all about being hot until I closed the book. Then I remembered.

Down by the water, I saw some kids building a sand castle.
"Do you think they'd let me help?" I asked.
"The best way to find out is to ask them," said Granny.
You know what? The kids said yes!
I'm good at making castles. I know how much water
to mix with the sand so it gets muddy, not drippy. And
I always find great things for trimming.

Our castle was big with lots of towers. I wanted to
build another castle and connect them both with a tunnel.

But the sun was going down, and one by one the kids were leaving. I said good-bye to them and went back up to Granny.

"Do we have to go home now?" I asked.

"Oh, no," said Granny. "This is when the beach gets pretty and quiet. And the birds come down."

She gave me crackers to feed them. I ate a couple and put the rest on top of the sand castle. I watched the birds swoop down to get them. They reached the crackers just in time before a big wave came and washed the castle away.

The wave got me wet, too. Suddenly, there were goose bumps on my skin. I started shivering all over.

I ran back up to the blanket.

"Guess what, Granny!" I said. "I'm c-c-c-cold."

"That's because the sun went down," said Granny, wrapping the blanket around us. "Tell me, how c-c-c-cold are you?"

I smiled. I knew this game.

"I'm colder than a Popsicle on a stick!" I said.

"I'm colder than a big, old snowlady!" said Granny.

"Colder than a turkey in the freezer!" I said. And I started trotting around the beach like a big, fat turkey.

"Trot on back here," said Granny. "We've got to go home."

So we rode the train back. And by the time we got to our stoop...

there was a cool evening breeze waiting to greet us.